Edward Eggleston

Mr. Blake's Walking Stick

A Christmas Story for Boys and Girls

Edward Eggleston

Mr. Blake's Walking Stick
A Christmas Story for Boys and Girls

ISBN/EAN: 9783337165796

Printed in Europe, USA, Canada, Australia, Japan

Cover: Foto ©Andreas Hilbeck / pixelio.de

More available books at **www.hansebooks.com**

MR. BLAKE'S

WALKING-STICK:

A Christmas Story for Boys and Girls.

By EDWARD EGGLESTON,

AUTHOR OF

"THE ROUND TABLE STORIES," "THE CHICKEN LITTLE STORIES,"
"STORIES TOLD ON A CELLAR DOOR." ETC

CHICAGO:
ADAMS, BLACKMER, & LYON PUBLISHING CO.
1872.

TO OUR

LITTLE SILVERHAIR.

Who used to listen to My Stories;

BUT WHO IS NOW

𝕷𝖎𝖘𝖙𝖊𝖓𝖎𝖓𝖌 𝖙𝖔 𝖙𝖍𝖊 𝕮𝖍𝖗𝖎𝖘𝖙𝖒𝖆𝖘 𝕾𝖙𝖔𝖗𝖎𝖊𝖘 𝖔𝖋 𝖙𝖍𝖊 𝕬𝖓𝖌𝖊𝖑𝖘,

THIS BOOK IS DEDICATED.

PREFACE.

I have meant to furnish a book that would serve for a Christmas present to Sunday-scholars, either from the school or from their teachers. I hope it is a story, however, appropriate to all seasons, and that it will enforce one of the most beautiful and one of the most frequently forgotten precepts of the Lord Jesus.

EDWARD EGGLESTON.

CONTENTS.

CHAPTER IX.

CHAPTER X

CHAPTER XI.

MR. BLAKE'S WALKING-STICK.

CHAPTER I.

THE WALKING-STICK WALKS.

SOME men carry canes. Some men make the canes carry them. I never could tell just what Mr. Blake carried his cane for. I am sure it did not often feel his weight. For he was neither old, nor rich, nor lazy.

He was a tall, straight man, who walked as if he loved to walk, with a cheerful tread that was good to see. I am sure he didn't carry the cane for show. It was not one of those little sickly yellow things, that some men nurse as tenderly as Miss Snooks nurses her lap-dog. It was a great black stick of solid ebony, with a box-wood head, and I think Mr. Blake carried it for company. And it had a face, like that of an old man, carved on one side of the box-wood head. Mr. Blake kept it ringing in a hearty way upon the pavement as he walked, and the boys would look up from their marbles when they heard it, and say: "There comes Mr. Blake, the minister!" And I think that nearly every invalid and poor person in Thornton knew the cheerful voice of the minister's stout ebony stick.

It was a clear, crisp, sunshiny morning in December. The leaves were all gone, and the long lines of white frame houses that were hid away in the thick trees during the summer, showed themselves standing in straight rows now that the trees were bare. And Purser, Pond & Co.'s great factory on the brook in the valley below was plainly to be seen, with its long rows of windows shining and shimmering in the brilliant sun, and its brick chimney reached up like the Tower of Babel, and poured out a steady stream of dense, black smoke.

It was just such a shining winter morning. Mr. Blake and his walking-stick were just starting out for a walk together. "It's a fine morning," thought the minister, as he shut the parsonage gate. And when he struck the cane sharply on the stones it answered him cheerily: "It's a fine morning!" The cane

always agreed with Mr. Blake. So they were able
to walk together, according to Scripture, because
they were agreed.

Just as he came round the corner the minister
found a party of boys waiting for him. They had
already heard the cane remarking that it was a fine
morning before Mr. Blake came in sight.

"Good morning! Mr. Blake," said the three
boys.

"Good morning, my boys; I'm glad to see you,"
said the minister, and he clapped "Old Ebony"
down on the sidewalk, and it said "I am glad to see
you."

"Mr. Blake!" said Fred White, scratching his
brown head and looking a little puzzled. "Mr.
Blake, if it ain't any harm — if you don't mind, you
know, telling a fellow, — a boy, I mean —" Just
here he stopped talking; for though he kept on
scratching vigorously, no more words would come;
and comical Sammy Bantam, who stood alongside,
whispered, "Keep a-scratching, Fred; the old cow
will give down after a while!"

Then Fred laughed, and the other boys, and the
minister laughed, and the cane could do nothing but
stamp its foot in amusement.

"Well, Fred," said the minister, "What is it? speak out." But Fred couldn't speak now for laughing, and Sammy had to do the talking himself. He was a stumpy boy, who had stopped off short; and you couldn't guess his age, because his face was so much older than his body.

"You see, Mr. Blake," said Sammy, "we boys wanted to know, — if there wasn't any harm in your telling, — why, we wanted to know what kind of a thing we are, going to have on Christmas at our Sunday-school."

"Well, boys, I don't know any more about it yet than you do. The teachers will talk it over at their next meeting. They have already settled some things, but I have not heard what."

"I hope it will be something good to eat," said Tommy Puffer. Tommy's body looked for all the world like a pudding-bag. It was an india-rubber pudding-bag, though. I shouldn't like to say that Tommy was a glutton. Not at all. But I am sure that no boy of his age could put out of sight, in the same space of time, so many dough-nuts, ginger-snaps, tea-cakes, apple-dumplings, pumpkin-pies, jelly-tarts, puddings, ice-creams, raisins, nuts, and other things of the sort. Other people stared at him in wonder. He was never too full to take anything that was offered him, and at parties his weak and foolish mother was always getting all she could to stuff Tommy with. So when Tommy said he hoped it would be something nice to eat, and rolled his soft lips about, as though he had a cream tart in his mouth, all the boys laughed, and Mr. Blake smiled. I think even the cane would have smiled if it had thought it polite.

"I hope it'll be something pleasant," said Fred Welch.

"So do I," said stumpy little Tommy Bantam.

"So do I, boys," said Mr. Blake, as he turned away; and all the way down the block Old Ebony kept calling back, "So do I, boys! so do I!"

Mr. Blake and his friend the cane kept on down the street, until they stood in front of a building that was called "The Yellow Row." It was a long, two-story frame building, that had once been inhabited by genteel people. Why they ever built it in that shape, or why they daubed it with yellow paint, is more than I can tell. But it had gone out of fashion, and now it was, as the boys expressed it, "seedy." Old hats and old clothes filled many of the places once filled by glass. Into one room of this row Mr. Blake entered, saying : —

" How are you, Aunt Parm'ly ? "

" Howd'y, Mr. Blake, howd'y ! I know'd you was a-comin', honey, fer I hyeard the sound of yer cane afore you come in. I'm mis'able these yer days, thank you. I'se got a headache, an' a backache, and a toothache in de boot."

I suppose the poor old colored woman meant to say that she had a toothache " to boot."

" You see, Mr. Blake, Jane's got a little sumpin to do now, and we can git bread enough, thank the Lord, but as fer coal, that's the hardest of all. We has to buy it by the bucketful, and that's mity high at fifteen cents a bucket. An' pears like we couldn't never git nothin' a-head on account of my roomatiz. Where de coal's to come from dis ere winter I don't know, cep de good Lord sends it down out of the sky : and I reckon stone-coal don't never come dat dar road."

After some more talk, Mr. Blake went in to see Peter Sitles, the blind broom-maker.

" I hyeard yer stick, preacher Blake," said Sitles. " That air stick o' yourn's better'n a whole rigimint of doctors fer the blues. An' I've been a havin' on the blues powerful bad, Mr. Blake, these yer last few days. I remembered what you was a-saying the last time you was here, about trustin' of the good Lord. But I've had a purty consid'able heartache under my jacket fer all that. Now, there's that Ben of mine," and here Sitles pointed to a restless little fellow of nine years old, whose pants had been patched and pieced until they had more colors than Joseph's coat. He was barefoot, ragged, and looked hungry, as some poor children always do. Their minds seem hungrier than their bodies. He was rocking a baby in an old cradle. "There's Ben," continued the blind man, "he's as peart a boy as you ever see, preacher Blake, ef I do say it as hadn't orter say it. Bennie hain't got no clothes. I can't beg. But Ben orter be in school." Here Peter Sitles choked a little.

"How's broom-making, Peter?" said the minister.

"Well, you see, it's the machines as is a-spoiling us. The machines make brooms cheap, and what can a blind feller like me do agin the machines with nothing but my fingers? 'Tain't no sort o' use to butt my head agin the machines, when I ain't got no eyes nother. It's like a goat trying its head on a locomotive. Ef I could only eddicate Peter and the other two, I'd be satisfied. You see, I never had no

2

book-larnin' myself, and I can't talk proper no more'n a cow can climb a tree."

" But, Mr. Sitles, how much would a broom-machine cost you? " asked the minister.

" More'n it's any use to think on. It'll cost seventy dollars, and if it cost seventy cents 'twould be jest exactly seventy cents more'n I could afford to pay. For the money my ole woman gits fer washin' don't go noways at all towards feedin' the four children, let alone buying me a machine."

The minister looked at his cane, but it did not answer him. Something must be done. The minister was sure of that. Perhaps the walking-stick was, too. But what?

That was the question.

The minister told Sitles good-bye, and started to make other visits. And on the way the cane kept crying out, "Something *must* be done, — something MUST be done, — something MUST be done," making the *must* ring out sharper every time. When Mr. Blake and the walking-stick got to the market-house, just as they turned off from Milk Street into the busier Main Street, the cane changed its tune and begun to say, " But what, — but *what*, — but WHAT, — but WHAT," until it said it so sharply

that the minister's head ached, and he put Old
Ebony under his arm, so that it couldn't talk any
more.   It was a way he had of hushing it up when
he wanted to think.

CHAPTER II.

LONG-HEADED WILLIE.

"DE biskits is cold, and de steaks is cold as — as — ice, and dinner's spiled!" said Curlypate, a girl about three years old, as Mr. Blake came in from his forenoon of visiting. She tried to look very much vexed and "put out," but there was always either a smile or a cry hidden away in her dimpled cheek.

"Pshaw! Curlypate," said Mr. Blake, as he put down his cane, "you don't scold worth a cent!" And he lifted her up and kissed her.

And then Mamma Blake smiled, and they all sat down to the table. While they ate, Mr. Blake told about his morning visits, and spoke of Parm'ly without coal, and Peter Sitles with no broom-machine, and described little Ben Sitles's hungry face, and told how he had visited the widow Martin, who had no sewing-machine, and who had to receive help from the overseer of the poor. The overseer told her that she must bind out her daughter, twelve years old, and her boy of ten, if she expected to have any help; and the mother's heart was just about broken at the thought of losing her children.

Now, while all this was taking place, Willie Blake, the minister's son, a boy about thirteen years of age, sat by the big porcelain water-pitcher, listening to all that was said. His deep blue eyes looked over the pitcher at his father, then at his mother, taking in all their descriptions of poverty with a wondrous pitifulness. But he did not say much. What went on in his long head I do not know, for his was one of those heads that projected forward and backward, and the top of which overhung the base, for all the world like a load of hay. Now and then his mother looked at him, as if she would like to see through his skull and read his thoughts. But I think she didn't see anything but the straight, silken, fine, flossy hair, silvery white, touched a little bit, — only a little, — as he turned it in looking from one to the other, with a tinge of what people call a golden, but what is really a sort of a pleasant straw color. He usually talked, and asked questions, and laughed like other boys; but now he seemed to be swallowing the words of his father and mother more rapidly even

than he did his dinner; for, like most boys, he ate
as if it were a great waste of time to eat.   But when
he was done he did not hurry off as eagerly as usual
to reading or to play.   He sat and listened.

"What makes you look so sober, Willie?" asked
Helen, his sister.

"What you thinkin', Willie?" said Curlypate,
peering through the pitcher handle at him.

"Willie," broke in his father, "mamma and I are
going to a wedding out at Sugar Hill" —

"Sugar Hill ; O my !" broke in Curlypate.

"Out at Sugar Hill," continued Mr. Blake, strok-
ing the Curlypate, "and as I have some calls to
make, we shall not be back till bedtime.   I am sorry
to keep you from your play this Saturday afternoon,
but we have no other housekeeper but you and
Helen.   See that the children get their suppers
early, and be careful about fire."

I believe to "be careful about fire" is the last
command that every parent gives to children on
leaving them alone.

Now I know that people who write stories are
very careful nowadays not to make their boys too
good.   I suppose that I ought to represent Willie as
"taking on" a good deal when he found that he

couldn't play all Saturday afternoon, as he had expected. But I shall not. For one thing, at least, in my story, is true ; that is, Willie. If I tell you that he is good you may believe it. I have seen him.

He only said, " Yes, sir."

Mrs. Blake did not keep a girl. The minister did not get a small fortune of a salary. So it happened that Willie knew pretty well how to keep house. He was a good brave boy, never ashamed to help his mother in a right manly way. He could wash dishes and milk the cow, and often, when mamma had a sick-headache, had he gotten a good breakfast, never forgetting tea and toast for the invalid.

So Sancho, the Canadian pony, was harnessed to the minister's rusty buggy, and Mr. and Mrs. Blake got in and told the children good-bye. Then Sancho started off, and had gone about ten steps, when he was suddenly reined up with a " Whoa ! "

" Willie ! " said Mr. Blake.

" Sir."

" Be careful about fire."

" Yes, sir."

And then old blackey-brown Sancho moved on in a gentle trot, and Willie and Helen and Richard

went into the house, where Curlypate had already
gone, and where they found her on tiptoe, with her
short little fingers in the sugar-bowl, trying in vain
to find a lump that would not go to pieces in the
vigorous squeeze that she gave it in her desire to
make sure of it.

So Willie washed the dishes, while Helen wiped
them, and Richard put them away, and they had a
merry time, though Willie had to soothe several
rising disputes between Helen and Richard.   Then
a glorious lot of wood was gotten in, and Helen
came near sweeping a hole in the carpet in her eager
desire to " surprise mamma." Curlypate went in
the parlor and piled things up in a wonderful way,
declaring that she, too, was going to " *susprise* mamma." And doubtless mamma would have felt no
little surprise if she could have seen the parlor after
Curlypate " put it to rights."

Later in the evening the cow was milked, and a
plain supper of bread and milk eaten.   Then Richard and Curlypate were put away for the night.
And presently Helen, who was bravely determined
to keep Willie company, found her head trying to
drop off her shoulders, and so she had to give up
to the " sand man," and go to bed.

CHAPTER III.

THE WALKING-STICK A TALKING STICK.

WILLIE was now all by himself. He put on more wood, and drew the rocking-chair up by the fire, and lay back in it. It was very still ; he could hear every mouse that moved. The stillness seemed to settle clear down to his heart. Presently a wagon went clattering by. Then, as the sound died away in the distance, it seemed stiller 'than ever. Willie tried to sleep ; but he couldn't. He kept listening ; and after all he was listening to nothing ; nothing but that awful clock, that would keep up such a tick-tick, tick-tick, tick-tick. The curtains were down, and Willie didn't dare to raise them, or to peep out. He could *feel* how dark it was out doors.

But presently he forgot the stillness. He fell to thinking of what Mr. Blake had said at dinner. He thought of poor old rheumatic Parm'ly, and her single bucket of coal at a time. He thought of the blind broom-maker who needed a broom-machine, and of the poor widow whose children must be taken away because the mother had no sewing-machine. All of these thoughts made the night seem dark, and they made Willie's heart heavy. But the thoughts kept him company.

Then he wished he was rich, and he thought if he were as rich as Captain Purser, who owned the mill, he would give away sewing-machines to all poor widows who needed them. But pshaw! what was the use of wishing? His threadbare pantaloons told him how far, off he was from being rich.

But he would go to the Polytechnic; he would become a civil engineer. He would make a fortune some day when he became celebrated. Then he would give widow Martin a sewing-machine. This was the nice castle in the air that Willie built. But just as he put on the last stone a single thought knocked it down.

What would become of the widow and her children while he was learning to be an engineer and making a fortune afterward? And where would he get the money to go to the Polytechnic? This last question Willie had asked every day for a year or two past.

Unable to solve this problem, his head grew tired, and he lay down on the lounge, saying to himself, " Something must be done ! "

" Something must be done ! " Willie was sure somebody spoke. He looked around. There was nobody in the room.

" Something *must* be done ! " This time he saw in the corner of the room, barely visible in the shadow, his father's cane. The voice seemed to come from that corner.

" Something MUST be done ! " Yes, it was the cane. He could see its yellow head, and the face on one side was toward him. How bright its eyes were ! It did not occur to Willie just then that there was anything surprising in the fact that the walking-stick had all at once become a talking stick.

" Something MUST be done ! " said the cane, lifting its one foot up and bringing it down with emphasis at the word must. Willie felt pleased that the little old man — I mean the walking-stick — should come to his help.

" I tell you what," said Old Ebony, hopping out of his shady corner ; " I tell you what," it said, and then stopped as if to reflect ; then finished by saying, " It's a shame ! "

Willie was about to ask the cane to what he referred, but he thought best to wait till Old Ebony got ready to tell of his own accord. But the walking-stick did not think best to answer immediately, but took entirely a new and surprising track. It actually went to quoting Scripture!

" My eyes are dim," said the cane, " and I never had much learning ; canes weren't sent to school when I was young. Won't you read the thirty-fifth verse of the twentieth chapter of Acts."

Willie turned to the stand and saw the Bible open at that verse. He did not feel surprised. It seemed natural enough to him. He read the verse, not aloud, but to himself, for Old Ebony seemed to hear his thoughts. He read : —

" Ye ought to support the weak, and to remember the words of the Lord Jesus, how he said, It is more blessed to give than to receive."

" Now," said the walking-stick, stepping or hopping up toward the lounge and leaning thoughtfully over the head of it, " Now, I say that it is a shame that when the birthday of that Lord Jesus, who gave himself away, and who said it is more blessed to give than to receive, comes round, all of you Sunday-school scholars are thinking only of what you are going to get."

Willie was about to say that they gave as well as received on Christmas, and that his class had already raised the money to buy a Bible Dictionary for their teacher. But Old Ebony seemed to guess his thought, and he only said, " And that's another shame ! "

Willie couldn't see how this could be, and he thought the walking-stick was using very strong language indeed. I think myself the cane spoke too sharply, for I don't think the harm lies in giving to and receiving from our friends, but in neglecting the poor. But you don't care what I think, you want to know what the cane said.

" I'm pretty well acquainted with Scripture," said Old Ebony, " having spent fourteen years in company with a minister. Now won't you please read the twelfth and thirteenth verses of the fourteenth chapter of " —

But before the cane could finish the sentence, Willie heard some one opening the door. It was his father. He looked round in bewilderment. The oil in the lamp had burned out, and it was dark. The fire was low, and the room chilly.

" Heigh-ho, Willie, my son," said Mr. Blake, " where's your light, and where's your fire. This is a cold reception. What have you been doing? "

"Listening to the cane talk," he replied ; and thinking what a foolish answer that was, he put on some more coal, while his mother, who was lighting the lamp, said he must have been dreaming. The walking-stick stood in its corner, face to the wall, as if it had never been a talking stick.

CHAPTER IV.

MR. BLAKE AGREES WITH THE WALKING-STICK.

EARLY on Sunday morning Willie awoke and began to think about Sitles, and to wish he had money to buy him a broom-machine. And then he thought of widow Martin. But all his thinking would do no good. Then he thought of what Old Ebony had said, and he wished he could know what that text was that the cane was just going to quote.

"It was," said Willie, "the twelfth and thirteenth verses of the fourteenth chapter of something. I'll see."

So he began with the beginning of the Bible, and looked first at Genesis xiv. 12, 13. But it was about the time when Abraham had heard of the capture of Lot and mustered his army to recapture him. He thought a minute.

"That can't be what it is," said Willie, "I'll look at Exodus."

In Exodus it was about standing still at the Red Sea and waiting for God's salvation. It might mean that God would deliver the poor. But that was not just what the cane was talking about. It was about giving gifts to friends. So he went on to Leviticus. But it was about the wave offering, and the sin offering, and the burnt offering. That was not it. And so he went from book to book until he had reached the twelfth and thirteenth verses of the fourteenth chapter of the book of Judges. He was just reading in that place about Samson's riddle, when his mamma called him to breakfast.

He was afraid to say anything about it at the table for fear of being laughed at. But he was full of what the walking-stick said. And at family worship his father read the twentieth chapter of Acts. When he came to the part about its being more blessed to give than to receive, Willie said, "That's what the cane said."

"What did you say?" asked his father.

"I was only thinking out loud," said Willie.

"Don't think out loud while I am reading," said Mr. Blake.

Willie did not find time to look any further for the other verses. He wished his father had happened on them instead of the first text which the cane quoted.

In church he kept thinking all the time about the cane. "Now what could it mean by the twelfth and thirteenth verses of the fourteenth chapter? There isn't anything in the Bible against giving away presents to one's friends. It was only a dream anyhow, and maybe there's nothing in it."

But he forgot the services, I am sorry to say, in his thoughts. At last Mr. Blake arose to read his text. Willie looked at him, but thought of what the cane said. But what was it that attracted his attention so quickly?

"The twelfth and thirteenth verses " —

"Twelfth and thirteenth!" said Willie to himself.

"Of the fourteenth chapter," said the minister.

"Fourteenth chapter!" said Willie, almost aloud.

"Of Luke."

Willie was all ears, while Mr. Blake read : "Then said he also to him that bade him, When thou makest a dinner or a supper, call not thy friends, nor thy brethren, neither thy kinsmen, nor thy rich neighbors, lest they also bid thee again, and a recompense be made thee. But when thou makest

3

a feast, call the poor, the maimed, the lame, the
blind."

" 'That's it!' " he said, half aloud, but his mother
jogged him.

The minister added the next verse also, and read:
" And thou shalt be blessed, for they cannot recompense thee ; for thou shalt be recompensed at the
resurrection of the just."

Willie had never listened to a sermon as he did
to that. He stopped two or three times to wonder
whether the cane had been actually about to repeat
his father's text to him, or whether he had not heard
his father repeat it at some time, and had dreamed
about it.

I am not going to tell you much about Mr.
Blake's sermon. It was a sermon that he and the
walking-stick had prepared while they were going
round among the poor. I think Mr. Blake did not
strike his cane down on the sidewalk for nothing.
Most of that sermon must have been hammered out
in that way, when he and the walking-stick were
saying, " Something must be done! " For that was
just what that sermon said. It told about the wrong
of forgetting, on the birthday of Christ, to do anything for the poor. It made everybody think. But

Mr. Blake did not know how much of that sermon went into Willie Blake's long head, as he sat there with his white full forehead turned up to his father.

CHAPTER V. .

THE FATHER PREACHES AND THE SON PRACTICES.

THAT afternoon, Willie was at Sunday-school long before the time. He had a plan.

"I'll tell you what, boys," said he, ".let's not give Mr. Marble anything this year; and let's ask him not to give us anything. Let's get him to put the money he would use for us with the money we should spend on a present for him, and give it to buy coal for Old Aunt Parm'ly."

"I mean to spend all my money on soft gum drops and tarts," said Tommy Puffer; "they're splendid!" and with that he began, as usual, to roll his soft lips together in a half chewing, half sucking manner, as if he had a half dozen cream tarts under his tongue, and two dozen gum drops in his cheeks.

"Tommy," said stumpy little Sammy Bantam, "it's a good thing you didn't live in Egypt, Tommy, in the days of Joseph."

"Why?" asked Tommy.

"Because," said Sammy, looking around the room absently, as if he hardly knew what he was going to say, "because, you see" — and then he opened a book and began to read, as if he had forgotten to finish the sentence.

"Well, why?" demanded Tommy, sharply.

"Well, because if Joseph had had to feed you during the seven years of plenty, there wouldn't have been a morsel left for the years of famine!"

The boys laughed as boys will at a good shot, and Tommy reddened a little and said, regretfully, that he guessed the Egyptians hadn't any doughnuts.

Willie did not forget his main purpose, but carried his point in his own class. He still had time to speak to some of the boys and girls in other classes. Everybody liked to do what Willie asked ; there was something sweet and strong in his blue eyes, eyes that "did not seem to have any bottom, they were so deep," one of the girls said. Soon there was an excitement in the school, and about the door ; girls and boys talking and discussing, but as soon as any opposition came up Willie's half-coaxing but decided way bore it down. I think he was much helped by Sammy's wit, which was all on his side. It was agreed, finally, that whatever scholars meant to give to teachers, or teachers to scholars, should go to the poor.

The teachers caught the enthusiasm, and were very much in favor of the project, for in the whole movement they saw the fruit of their own teaching.

The superintendent had been detained, and was surprised to find the school standing in knots about the room. He soon called them to order, and expressed his regrets that they should get into such disorder. There was a smile on all faces, and he saw that there was something more in the apparent disorder than he thought. After school it was fixed that each class should find its own case of poverty. The young men's and the young women's Bible classes undertook to supply Sitles with a broom-machine, a class of girls took Aunt Parm'ly under their wing, other classes knew of other cases of need, and so each class had its hands full. But Willie could not get any class to see that Widow Martin had a sewing-machine. That was left for his own; and how should a class of eight boys do it?

CHAPTER VI.

SIXTY-FIVE DOLLARS.

ILLIE took the boys into the parsonage. They figured on it. There were sixty-five dollars to be raised to buy the machine. The seven boys were together, for Tommy Puffer had gone home. He said he didn't feel like staying, and Sammy Bantam thought he must be a little hungry.

Willie attacked the problem, sixty-five dollars. Toward that amount they had three dollars and a half that they had intended to spend on a present for Mr. Marble. That left just sixty-one dollars and fifty cents to be raised. Willie ran across the street and brought Mr. Marble. He said he had made up his mind to give the boys a book apiece, and that each book would cost a dollar. It was rather more than he could well afford ; but as he had intended to give eight dollars for their presents, and as he was pleased with their unselfish behavior, he would make it ten.

"Good!" said Charley Somerset, who always saw the bright side of things, "that makes it all, except fifty-one dollars and a half."

"Yes," said Sammy Bantam, "and you're eleven feet high, lacking a couple of yards!"

Willie next called his father in, and inquired how much his Christmas present was to cost.

"Three and a half," said his father.

"That's a lot! Will you give me the money instead?"

"Yes; but I meant to give you a Life of George Stephenson, and some other books on engineering."

This made Willie think a moment; but seeing the walking-stick in the corner, he said: "Mrs. Martin must have a machine, and that three and a half makes seventeen dollars. How to get the other forty-eight is the question."

Mr. Blake and Mr. Marble both agreed that the boys could not raise so much money, and should not undertake it. But Willie said there was nobody to do it, and he guessed it would come somehow. The other boys, when they came to church that evening, told Willie that their presents were commuted for money also; so they had twenty-five dollars toward the amount. But that was the end of it, and there were forty dollars yet to come !

Willie lay awake that night, thinking. Mr. Marble's class could not raise the money. All the other classes had given all they could. And the teachers would each give in their classes. And they had raised all they could spare besides to buy nuts and candy ! Good ! That was just it; they would do without candy !

At school the next morning, Willie's white head was bobbing about eagerly. He made every boy and girl sign a petition, asking the teachers not to give them any nuts or candy. They all signed except Tommy Puffer. He said it was real mean not to have any candy. They might just as well not have any Sunday-school, or any Christmas either. But seeing a naughty twinkle in Sammy Bantam's eye, he waddled away, while Sammy fired a shot after him, by remarking that, if Tommy had been one of the Shepherds in Bethlehem, he wouldn't have listened to the angels till he had inquired if they had any lemon-drops in their pockets !

That night the extra Teachers' Meeting was held, and in walked white-headed Willie with stunted Sammy Bantam at his heels to keep him in countenance. When their petition was presented, Miss Belden, who sat near Willie, said, "Well done! Willie."

"But I protest," said Mrs. Puffer, — who was of about as handsome a figure as her son, — "I protest against such an outrage on the children. My Tommy's been a-feeling bad about it all day. It'll break his heart if he don't get some candy."

Willie was shy, but for a moment he forgot it, and, turning his intelligent blue eyes on Mrs. Puffer, he said, —

"It will break Mrs. Martin's heart if her children are taken away from her."

"Well," said Mrs. Puffer, "I always did hear that the preacher's boy was the worst in the parish, and I won't take any impudence. My son will join the Mission School, where they aren't too stingy to give him a bit of candy!" And Mrs. Puffer left, and everybody was pleased.

"Willie got the money; but the teachers had counted on making up their festival mostly with cakes and other dainties, contributed by families. So that the candy money was only sixteen dollars, and Willie was yet a long way off from having the amount he needed. Twenty-four dollars were yet wanting.

CHAPTER VII.

THE WIDOW AND THE FATHERLESS.

THE husband of widow Martin had been killed by a railroad accident. The family were very poor. Mrs. Martin could sew, and she could have sustained her family if she had had a machine. But fingers are not worth much against iron wheels. And so, while others had machines, Mrs. Martin could not make much without one. She had been obliged to ask help from the overseer of the poor.

Mr Lampeer, the overseer, was a hard man. He had not skill enough to detect impostors, and so he had come to believe that everybody who was poor was rascally. He had but one eye, and he turned his head round in a curious way to look at you out of it. That dreadful one eye always seemed to be going to shoot. His voice had not a chord of tenderness in it, but was in every way harsh and hard. It

was said that he had been a schoolmaster once. I
pity the scholars.

Widow Martin lived — if you could call it living
— in a tumble-down looking house, that would not
have stood many earthquakes. She had tried dili-
gently to support her family and keep them together ;
but the wolf stood always at the door. Sewing by
hand did not bring in quite money enough to buy
bread and clothes for four well children, and pay
the expenses of poor little Harry's sickness ; for all
through the summer and fall Harry had been sick.
At last the food was gone, and there was nothing
to buy fuel with. Mrs. Martin had to go to the
overseer of the poor.

She was a little, shy, hard-working woman, this
Mrs. Martin ; so when she took her seat among the
paupers of every sort in Mr. Lampeer's office, and
waited her turn, it was with a trembling heart. She
watched the hard man, who didn't mean to be so
hard, but who couldn't tell the difference between
a good face and a counterfeit ; she watched him as
he went through with the different cases, and her
heart beat every minute more and more violently.
When he came to her he broke out with —

"What's *your* name ? " in a voice that sounded

for all the world as if he were accusing her of robbing a safe.

"Sarah Martin," said the widow, trembling with terror, and growing red and white in turns. Mr. Lampeer, who was on the lookout for any sign of guiltiness, was now sure that Mrs. Martin could not be honest.

"Where do you live?" This was spoken with a half sneer.

"In Slab Alley," whispered the widow, for her voice was scared out of her.

"How many children have you got?"

Mrs. Martin gave him the list of her five, with their ages, telling him of little Harry, who was six years old and an invalid.

"Your oldest is twelve and a girl. I have a place for her, and, I think, for the boy, too. You must bind them out. Mr. Slicker, the landlord of the Farmers' Hotel, will take the girl, and I think James Sweeny will take the boy to run errands about the livery stable. I'll send you some provisions and coal to-day; but you must let the children go. I'll come to your house in a few days. Don't object; I won't hear a word. If you're as poor as you let on to be, you'll be glad enough to get your young ones into places where they'll get enough to eat. That's all, not a word, now." And he turned to the next applicant, leaving the widow to go home with her heart *so* cold.

Let Susie go to Slicker's tavern! What kind of a house would it be without her? Who would attend to the house while she sewed? And what would become of her girl in such a place? And then to send George, who had to wait on Harry, to send him away forever was to shut out all hope of ever being in better circumstances. Then she could not sew, and the children could never help her. God pity the people that fall into the hands of public charity!

The next few days wore heavily on with the widow. What to do she did not know. At night she scarcely slept at all. When she did drop into a sleep, she dreamed that her children were starving, and woke in fright. Then she slept again, and dreamed that a one-eyed robber had gotten in at the window, and was carrying off Susie and George. At last morning came. The last of the food was eaten for breakfast, and widow Martin sat down to wait. Her mind was in a horrible state of doubt. To starve to death together, or to give up her chil-

dren ! That was the question which many a poor
mother's heart has had to decide. Mrs. Martin soon
became so nervous she could not sew. She could
not keep back the tears, and when Susie and George
put their arms about her neck and asked what was
the matter, it made the matter worse. It was the
day before Christmas. The sleigh-bells jingled mer-
rily. Even in Slab Alley one could hear sounds of
joy at the approaching festivities. But there was
no joy in Widow Martin's house or heart. The
dinner hour had come and passed. The little children were hungry. And yet Mrs. Martin had not
made up her mind.

At the appointed time Lampeer came. He took
out the two indentures with which the mother was
to sign away all right to her two eldest children. It
was in vain that the widow told him that if she lost
them she could do no work for her own support, and
must be forever a pauper. Lampeer had an idea
that no poor person had a right to love children.
Parental love was, in his eyes, or his eye, an expen-
sive luxury that none but the rich should indulge in.

"Mrs. Martin," he said, "you may either sign
these indentures, by which your girl will get a good
place as a nurse and errand girl for the tavern-

keeper's wife, and your boy will have plenty to eat and get to be a good hostler, or you and your brats may starve!" With that he took his hat and opened the door.

"Stop!" said Mrs. Martin, "I must have medicine and food, or Harry will not live till Sunday. I will sign."

The papers were again spread out. The poor-master jerked the folds out of them impatiently, in a way that seemed to say, "You keep me an unconscionable long time about a very small matter."

When the papers were spread out, Mrs. Martin's two oldest children, who began to understand what was going on, cried bitterly. Mrs. Martin took the pen and was about to sign. But it was necessary to have two witnesses, and so Lampeer took his hat and called a neighbor-woman, for the second witness.

Mrs. Martin delayed the signature as long as she could. But seeing no other help, she took up the pen. She thought of Abraham with the knife in his hand. She hoped that an angel would call out of heaven to her relief. But as there was no voice from heaven, she dipped the pen in the ink.

Just then some one happened to knock at the door, and the poor woman's nerves were so weak that she let the pen fall, and sank into a chair. Lampeer, who stood near the door, opened it with an impatient jerk, and — did the angel of deliverance enter?

It was only Willie Blake and Sammy Bantam.

CHAPTER VIII.

SHARPS AND BETWEENS.

ET us go back. We left Willie awhile ago puzzling over that twenty-four dollars. After many hours of thought and talk with Sammy about how they should manage it, two gentlemen gave them nine dollars, and so there was but fifteen more to be raised. But that fifteen seemed harder to get than the fifty they had already gotten. At last Willie thought of something. They would try the sewing-machine man. Mr. Sharps would throw off fifteen dollars.

But they did not know Mr. Sharps. Though he made more than fifteen dollars on the machine, he hated to throw anything off. He was always glad to put on. Sammy described him by saying that " Mr. Sharps was not for-giving but he was for-getting."

They talked; they told the story; they begged. Mr. Sharps really could not afford to throw off a cent. He was poor. Taxes were high. He gave a great deal. (I do not know what he called a great deal. He had been to church three times in a year, and twice he had put a penny in the plate. I suppose Mr. Sharps thought that a great deal. And so it was, for him, poor fellow.) And then the butcher had raised the price of meat ; and he had to pay twenty-three dollars for a bonnet for his daughter. Really, he was too poor. So the boys went away down-hearted.

But Sammy went straight to an uncle of his, who was one of the editors of the *Thornton Daily Bugle.* After a private talk with him he started back to Mr. Sharps. Willie followed Sammy this time. What Sammy had in his head Willie could not make out.

" I'll fix him ! " That was the only word Sammy uttered on the way back.

" Now, Mr. Sharps," he began, " my uncle's name is Josiah Penn. Maybe you know him. He's one of the editors of the *Thornton Daily Bugle.* I've been talking with him. If you let me have a Feeler and Stilson sewing-machine for fifty dollars, I will have a good notice put in the *Daily Bugle.*"

Mr. Sharps whistles a minute. He thought he could not do it. No, he was too poor.

" Well, then, Willie," said Sammy, " we'll go

across the street and try the agent of the Hillrocks
and Nibbs machine. I think Mr. Betweens will
take my offer."

"O!" said Mr. Sharps, "you don't want that
machine. It's only a single thread, and it will ravel,
and — well — you don't want that."

"Indeed, my mother says there isn't a pin to
choose between them," said Sammy; "and I can
give Mr. Betweens just as good a notice as I could
give you."

"Very well, take the machine for fifty dollars. I
do it just out of pity for the widow, you know. I
never could stand by and see suffering and not re-
lieve it. You won't forget about that notice in the
Daily Bugle, though, will you?"

No, Sammy wouldn't forget.

It was now the day before Christmas, and the
boys thought they had better get the machine down
there.

So they found Billy Horton, who belonged to
their class, and who drove an express wagon, and
told him about it. He undertook to take it down.
But first, he drove around the town and picked up
all the boys of the class, that they might share in
the pleasure.

Meantime, a gentleman who had heard of Willie's efforts, gave him a five dollar bill for widow Martin. This Willie invested in provisions, which he instructed the grocer to send to the widow.

He and Sammy hurried down to wiaow Martin's, and got there, as I told you in the last chapter, just as she was about to sign away all right, title, and interest in two of the children whom God had given her ; to sign them away at the command of the hard Mr. Lampeer, who was very much irritated that he should be interrupted just at the moment when he was about to carry the point ; for he loved to carry a point better than to eat his breakfast.

CHAPTER IX.

THE ANGEL STAYS THE HAND.

HEN the boys came in, they told the widow that they wished to speak with little sick Harry. They talked to Harry awhile, without noticing what was going on in the other part of the room.

Presently Willie felt his arm pulled. Looking round, he saw Susie's tearful face. "Please don't let mother give me and George away." Somehow all the children in school had the habit of coming to this long-headed Willie for help, and to him Susie came.

That word of Susie's awakened Willie. Up to that moment he had not thought what Mr. Lampeer was there for. Now he saw Mrs. Martin holding the pen with trembling hand. and making motions in the air preparatory to writing her name. Most people not used to writing, write in the air before they touch the paper. When Willie saw this, he flew

across the room and thrust his hand upon the place
where the name ought to be, saying, —

" Don't do that, Mrs. Martin ! Don't give away
your children ! "

Poor woman! the pen dropped from her hand as
the knife had dropped from Abraham's. She grasped
Willie's arm, saying, —

" How can I help it ?   Do tell me ! "

But Lampeer had grasped the other arm, and
broke out with —

" You rogue, what do you mean ? "

Willie's fine blue eyes turned quickly into Lampeer's one muddy eye.

" Let go ! " he said, very quietly but very deter-
minedly, " don't strike me, or my father will take
the law on you."

Lampeer let go.

Just then the groceries came, and a minute later,
Billy Horton's wagon drove up with the machine,
and all the other boys, who came in and shook hands
with the poor but delighted mother and her children.
I cannot tell you any more about that scene. I only
know that Lampeer went out angry and muttering.

CHAPTER X.

TOMMY PUFFER.

ILLIE was happy that night. He went down to the festival at the Mission. There was Tommy Puffer's soft, oyster-like body among the scholars of the Mission. He was waiting for something good. His mouth and eyes were watering. He looked triumphantly at the boys from the other school. They wouldn't get anything so nice. The superintendent announced that no boy's name would be called for a paper bag of "refreshments" but those who had been present two Sundays. And so poor starving Tommy Puffer had to carry his pudding-bag of a body home again without a chance to give it an extra stuffing.

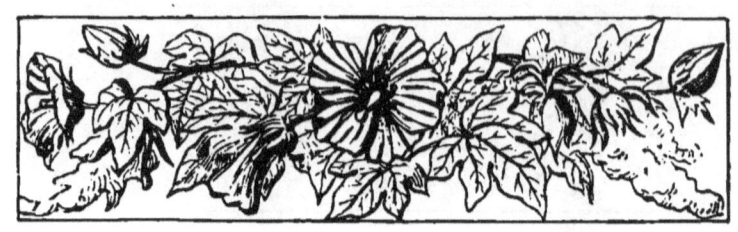

CHAPTER XI.

AN ODD PARTY.

 CANNOT tell you about the giving of the broom-machine to the blind broom-maker; of the ton of coal to Parm'ly, and of all the other things that happened on Christmas Day when the presents were given. I must leave these things out. As for Aunt Parm'ly, she said she did not know, but dat dare coal seemed like it come from de sky.

But there was an ample feast yet for the boys at the Sunday-school, for many biscuits, and cakes, and pies had been baked. But every time Willie looked at the walking stick he thought of " the poor, the maimed, the lame, and the blind." And so he and Sammy Bantam soon set the whole school, teachers and all, a-fire with the idea of inviting in the inmates of the county poor-house. It was not half so hard to persuade the members of the school to do this as it was to coax them to the first move ; for when people have found out how good it is to do good, they like to do good again.

Such a company it was ! There was old crazy Newberry, who had a game-bag slung about his neck, and who imagined that the little pebbles in it were of priceless value. Old Dorothy, who was nearly eighty, and who, thanks to the meanness of the authorities, had not tasted any delicacy, not so much as a cup of tea, since she had been in the alms-house ; and there were half-idiots, and whole idiots, and sick people, and crippled people, armless people and legless people, blind people and deaf. Such an assortment of men, women, and little children, you cannot often find. They were fed with the good things provided for the Sunday-school children, much to the disgust of Tommy Puffer and his mother. For Tommy was bent on getting something to eat here.

There were plenty of people who claimed the credit of suggesting this way of spending the Christmas. But Willie did not say anything about it, for he remembered what Christ had said about blowing a trumpet before you. But I think Sammy Bantam trumpeted Willie's fame enough.

It would be hard to tell who enjoyed the Christ-

mas the most.   But I think the givers found it more
blessed than the receivers.   What talk Mr. Blake
heard in his rounds I cannot tell.   If you want to
know, you must ask the Old Ebony.

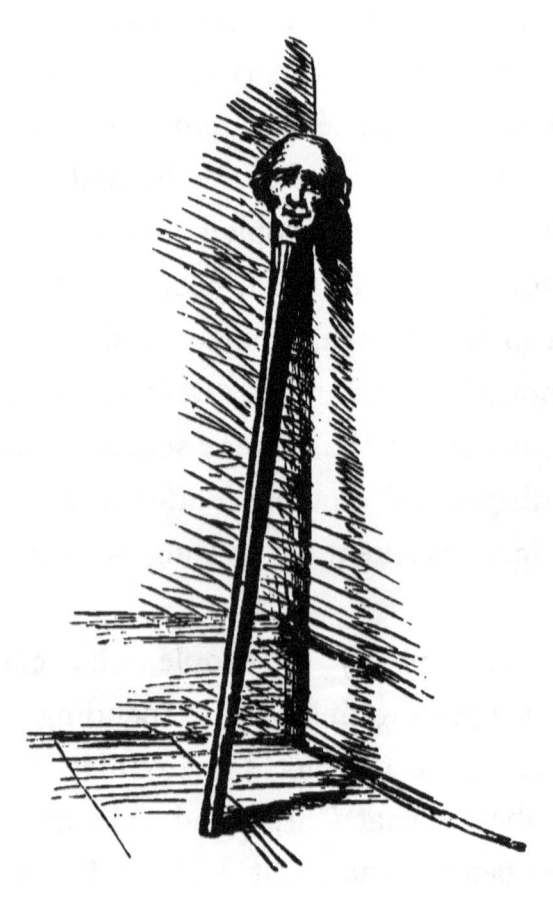